MRS PEPPERPOT
AND THE
BLUEBERRIES

MRS PEPPERPOT AND THE BLUEBERRIES
A RED FOX BOOK 978 1 849 41647 4

First published in Great Britain as "Mrs Pepperpot and the Bilberries" by Hutchinson, 1990
an imprint of Random House Children's Publishers UK
A Random House Group Company

This edition published 2013

1 3 5 7 9 10 8 6 4 2

Text copyright © Alf Prøysen, 1958
Illustrations copyright © Hilda Offen, 2013
English translation copyright © Hutchinson Children's Books, 1990
Text abridgement copyright © Random House Children's Publishers UK, 2013

Red Fox Books are published by Random House Children's Publishers UK,
61–63 Uxbridge Road, London W5 5SA

www.**randomhousechildrens**.co.uk
www.**randomhouse**.co.uk

Addresses for companies within The Random House Group Limited can be found at:
www.randomhouse.co.uk/offices.htm

THE RANDOM HOUSE GROUP Limited Reg. No. 954009

A CIP catalogue record for this book is available from the British Library.

Printed in China

The Random House Group Limited supports the Forest Stewardship Council® (FSC®), the leading
international forest-certification organisation. Our books carrying the FSC label are printed on FSC®-certified paper.
FSC is the only forest-certification scheme supported by the leading environmental organisations, including Greenpeace.
Our paper procurement policy can be found at www.randomhouse.co.uk/environment

FSC
www.fsc.org

MIX
Paper from
responsible sources
FSC® C104723

MRS PEPPERPOT
AND THE BLUEBERRIES

ALF PRØYSEN ❖ **HILDA OFFEN**

RED FOX

Mr Pepperpot was in a bad mood – he had been in it for days – and Mrs Pepperpot simply didn't know how to get him out of it. She put flowers on the table and cooked him his favourite dish; fried bacon with macaroni cheese. But it was all no use; Mr Pepperpot just went on moping.

"I don't know what's the matter with him," sighed Mrs Pepperpot. "Perhaps he's pining for pancakes." So she made him a big pile of pancakes.

When her husband came in for dinner his face lit up at the sight of them, but as soon as he'd sat down and picked up his knife and fork to start eating, his face fell again; he was as glum as before.

"Ah well!" he said, staring up at the ceiling, "I suppose it's too much to expect."

"I've had enough of this!" cried Mrs Pepperpot. "You tell me what's wrong, or I'll *shrink*, so I will!" (You remember that Mrs Pepperpot had a habit of shrinking to the size of a pepperpot, though not usually, I'm afraid, when she *wanted* to, but at the most inconvenient moments.) "You have something on your mind, that's quite clear," she went on. "Now even pancakes can't cheer you up."

"Pancakes are all right," nodded Mr Pepperpot, "but couldn't we sometimes have a bit of blueberry jam with the pancakes, instead of just eating them plain?" And Mr Pepperpot gave a great sigh.

At last she understood; it *was* a very long time since they'd had
blueberry jam, and that was what he had been missing.

"Well, if that's all you want, I'll go and pick some blueberries
this very minute," said Mrs Pepperpot, and she snatched a
bucket from a hook on the wall and rushed out of the door.

She walked rather fast, and as she walked she talked to herself:
"I've got the silliest husband alive," she muttered.

In no time at all she reached the spot in the forest where the
blueberries grew. She put her bucket under a bush and started
picking into the cup she had in her apron pocket.

Every time the cup was full she emptied it into the bucket. Cup after cup went in, until the bucket needed only one more cup to be quite full. But then, just as she had picked the last blueberry into the cup, lo and behold! She shrank to the size of a pepperpot.

"Now we're in a jam, that's certain, and I don't mean blueberry jam!" said the little old woman, who now had a tiny voice like a mouse. "Still, I expect I can manage to get the cup as far as the bucket if I push and pull hard enough."

So she crooked her arm through the handle and dragged the cup along. It was very hard at first, but then she came to an ant-path made of slippery pine needles and here it was much easier, because the cup could slide along it. And all the time little ants and big ants kept scuttling to and fro beside her.

She tried to talk to them.

"How d'you do, ants," she said. "Hard at work, I see. Yes, there's always plenty to do and that's a fact." But the ants were far too busy to answer.

"Couldn't you stop for a minute and talk to me?" she asked. But they just hurried on. "Well, I shall have to talk to myself; then I won't be disturbing anybody." And she sat down with her back leaning against the cup.

As she sat there, she suddenly felt something breathe down her neck; she turned round, and saw a fox standing there waving his tail in a friendly sort of way.

"Hello, Mr Fox. Are you out for a stroll?" said Mrs Pepperpot. "Lucky you don't know my hens are … Oh dear! I nearly let my tongue run away with me!"

"Where did you say your hens were, Mrs Pepperpot?" asked the fox in his silkiest voice.

"That would be telling, wouldn't it?" said Mrs Pepperpot. "But, as you see, I'm rather busy just now, I've got to get this cup of blueberries hauled over to the bucket somehow, so I haven't time to talk to you."

"I'll carry the cup for you," said the fox, as polite as could be. "Then you can talk while we walk."

"Thanks very much," said Mrs Pepperpot. "As I was saying, my hens are … There now! I nearly said it again!"

The fox smiled encouragingly, "Just go on talking, it doesn't matter what you say to me."

"I'm not usually one to gossip, but somehow it seems so easy to talk about my hens being … Goodness, why don't I keep my mouth shut? Anyway, there's the bucket. So, if you would be so kind and set the cup down beside it I'll tell you where my hens are."

"That's right," said the fox. "Your hens will be quite safe with me."

"They certainly will!" laughed Mrs Pepperpot, "for they're all away! They were broody, so I lent them to the neighbours to hatch out their eggs."

Then the fox saw he had been tricked, and he was so ashamed he slunk away into the forest and hid himself.

"Ha, ha, ha! That was a fine trick you played on the fox!" said a voice quite close to Mrs Pepperpot. She looked up and there stood a wolf towering over her.

"Well, if it isn't Mr Wolf!" said Mrs Pepperpot, swallowing hard to keep her courage. "The ve-very person I need. You can help me tip this cup of blueberries into the bucket."

"Oh no, you can't fool me like you did the fox," said the wolf.

"I'm not trying to fool you at all," said Mrs Pepperpot; she had had a good idea and was no longer afraid. "You'd better do as I say or I'll send for One-eye Threadless!"

The wolf laughed. "I've heard many old wives' tales but I've never heard that one before!"

"It's not an old wives' tale," said Mrs Pepperpot indignantly, "and I'm not just an old wife – I'm Mrs Pepperpot who can shrink and grow again in a flash. One-eye Threadless is my servant."

"Ha, ha! I'd like to see that servant of yours!" laughed the wolf.

"Very well, stick your nose into my apron pocket here and you'll meet him," said Mrs Pepperpot. So the wolf put his nose in her apron pocket and pricked it very severely on a needle she kept there.

"Ow, ow!" he shouted and started running towards the forest. But Mrs Pepperpot called him back at once, "Come here! You haven't done your job yet, empty that cup into that bucket, and don't you dare spill a single berry, or I'll send for One-eye Threadless to prick you again!"

The wolf didn't dare disobey her, but as soon as he had emptied the cup into the bucket he ran like the fox to the forest to hide.

Mrs Pepperpot had a good laugh as she watched him go, but then she heard something rustle near the bucket.

This time it was the big brown bear himself.

"Dear me! What an honour!" said Mrs Pepperpot in a shaky voice, and she curtsied so low she nearly disappeared into the bushes. "Has the fine weather tempted Your Majesty out for a walk?"

"Yes," growled the big brown bear and went on sniffing at the bucket.

"How very fortunate for me! As Your Majesty can see, I've picked a whole bucket of berries, but it's not very safe for a little old woman like myself to walk in the forest alone. Could I ask Your Majesty to carry the bucket out to the road for me?"

"I don't know about that," said the bear. "I like the blueberries myself."

"Yes, of course, but you're not like the rest of them, Your Majesty, you wouldn't rob a poor little old woman like me!"

"Blueberries, that's what I want!" said the bear, and put his head down to start eating.

In a flash Mrs Pepperpot had jumped on his neck and started tickling him behind the ears.

"What are you doing?" asked the bear.

"I'm just tickling your ears for you," answered Mrs Pepperpot. "Doesn't it feel good?"

"Good? It's almost better than eating the berries!" said the bear.

"Well, if Your Majesty would be so kind as to carry the bucket, I could be tickling Your Majesty's ears all the way," said the artful Mrs Pepperpot.

"Oh, very well then," grumbled the bear.

When they reached the road the bear put the bucket down very carefully on a flat stone.

"Many, many thanks, Your Majesty," said Mrs Pepperpot as she made another deep curtsey.

"Thank *you*," said the bear, and shuffled off into the forest.

When the bear had gone Mrs Pepperpot became her usual size again, so she picked up the bucket and hurried homeward.

"It's really not very difficult to look after yourself, even when you're only the size of a pepperpot," she told herself. "As long as you know how to tackle the people you meet. Cunning people must be tricked, cowardly ones must be frightened, and the big, strong ones must have their ears tickled."

"As for bad-tempered husbands, the only thing to do with them is to give them blueberry jam with their pancakes."